Violet's Magical Journey:
A Story of Adoption

Written by Aiyana Sequana
Illustrated by Mary Toews

Published by Waldorf Publishing
2140 Hall Johnson Road
#102-345
Grapevine, Texas 76051
www.WaldorfPublishing.com

Violet's Magical Journey:
A Story of Adoption

ISBN: 978-1-944781-38-5

Library of Congress Control Number: 2016930006

Once upon a time there was a young fairy named Violet.

She was a very independent and high-spirited fairy who loved to play and explore. She was also very curious.

It came to pass one day that Violet flew over two human children. The children were doing something that seemed very odd to her. They were gliding along the ground with shoes that had wheels on them. And they were giggling as they did so, even when they fell down on the ground. They would just pick themselves up, dust themselves off, and glide off again. There didn't seem to be any purpose to this. But they were clearly enjoying what they were doing.

As it was time to go home, Violet turned around and flew away, back to the fairy realm. But Violet could not stop thinking about the human children and all the fun that they seemed to be having.

So she decided to go to the wizard of the castle to ask him about what she had seen as he was the smartest creature in all the land. He would surely know what the humans had been doing.

When Violet arrived at the wizard's chamber she said, "I saw something today that I don't understand. I was hoping that you could help me out."

The wizard said, "As I am the smartest creature in all the land, I will surely be able to help."

So Violet proceeded to tell the wizard about the humans she had seen and what they had been doing. The wizard chuckled and then said, "The humans were skating!"

"But why?" asked Violet.

"Because it is fun," answered the wizard.

"Fun? No other purpose?" asked Violet.

"Fun is its own purpose," replied the wizard.

He would say no more and shooed Violet out of his chamber.

Violet thought and thought and thought about
what the wizard had said.

The more she thought about it the more she
liked the notion of fun, though she still didn't
understand how it could be its own purpose.

The next day she went back to the wizard's chamber because she had one more question for him.

"Could I learn to skate?" she asked.

"Oh, no," answered the wizard. "Fairies fly. Only humans skate — probably because they cannot fly."

As before, he would say no more and shooed Violet out of his chamber.

Violet thought and thought some more about what the wizard had said. Finally, she could stand it no longer and flew back to the wizard's chamber. "Could I become a human?" asked Violet.

The wizard thought a long time before he answered her. "Well, hmmm, yes, you could. But you need to understand that fairy years and human years are very different — and humans do not live as long as fairies. So I wouldn't recommend it."

"I don't care!" responded Violet. "I want to have fun and find out how it is its own purpose."

"Well, you would also need to arrive in a slightly different manner than most children," said the wizard hesitantly.

"And how is that?" asked Violet.

"You would have a mother and father whose gift to you would be to open the door at the end of the rainbow bridge and place you, filled with life and joy, upon the earth. That would be all that they would give you.

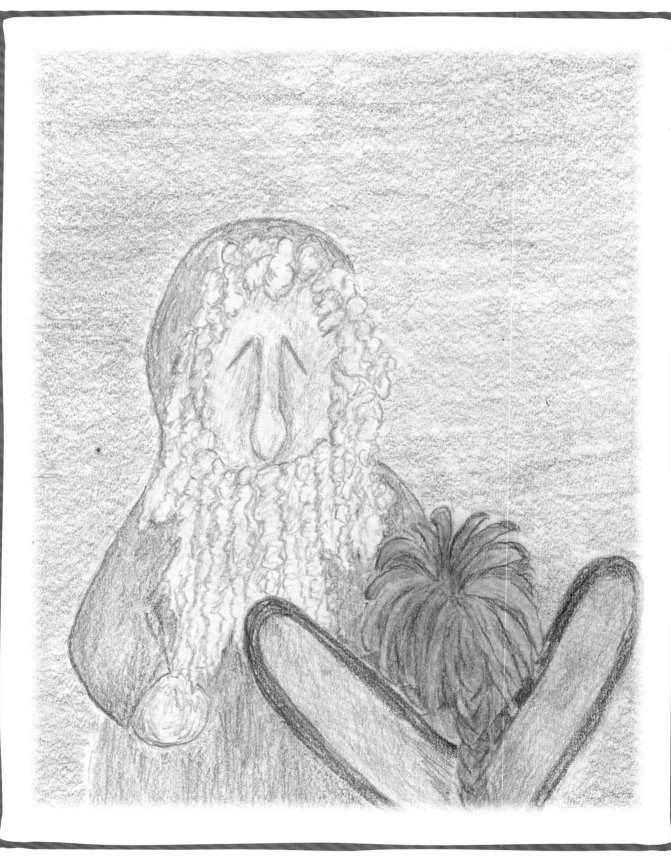

And then you would have a mother and a father who could not open the rainbow door or fill you with that first life, but who could give you a loving home where you could grow in joy and learn all you need to know to love the earth," responded the wizard.

"Sounds perfect!" said Violet. "Let's do it."

And so they did.

Violet went to dreamland and rocked in a little
boat for nine months.

At the end of that time a beautiful colored
rainbow stretched from heaven to earth, and on
it she came down to earth as a tiny baby.

And she was named Melanie.

Her mother and her father loved her very much
and took care of her —

and she began to grow.

When Melanie was 6 and ¾ she learned to skate.

One day, while she was skating, she came upon two children skating. Suddenly she remembered that she had once been a fairy and that her name had been Violet.

Just as suddenly, she remembered what the wizard had said about fun being its own purpose. And then she finally understood!

Fun needs no purpose!

It was enough to just experience fun. She was so excited that she jumped for joy!!

She realized right then that the wizard was not the smartest creature in all the land after all. She knew that she was — for she had made the wise choice to become a human child.

And so it was if it ever was.

Author Bio

Aiyana Sequana is a California native who obtained her degree in Rhetoric and has always been fascinated by the power of the written word. More recently she has become a student of Compassionate Communication, and learning how a shift in the way we think about things can lead to better human connection.

Since having become an adoptive mother, Aiyana is particularly sensitive to the dynamics surrounding adoption. Out of this came VIOLET, which was originally a puppet show that Aiyana scripted for her daughter's fifth birthday. Recently, her daughter turned 21; the puppet show has now resurfaced and evolved into a book.